JUST-IN-TIME JOEY

written and illustrated by

LEONARD SHORTALL

William Morrow and Company
New York 1973

Inquiries should be addressed to William Morrow and Company, Inc.,
105 Madison Ave., New York, N.Y. 10016.
Printed in the United States of America.
1 2 3 4 5 77 76 75 74 73

Shortall, Leonard W.
   Just-in-time Joey.

   SUMMARY: Joey's quick thinking saves a healthy
tree from being cut down for having Dutch elm disease.
   I. Title.
PZ7.S55878Ju   [E]   72-12951
ISBN 0-688-20073-7
ISBN 0-688-30073-1 (lib bdg.)

One summer when Joey was six
he went to visit his grandmother.
She lived in a big, old house
in a small country town. His
mother and father were going to
be away on a long trip.

Joey liked his grandmother's house. He liked the wide porches that went nearly all the way around it. He liked his room that was in a dormer way up on the top floor. When he leaned out the window, he could touch the roof on each side. In front there was a giant elm tree, and he looked out right into the green leaves. Tall trees grew on either side of the road as far as Joey could see.

On the first morning of his visit, Joey's grandmother asked him to run an errand for her.

"Would you please go to Mr. Hardy's house?" she said. "I need his hatchet to cut tomato stakes this afternoon." She told him that there was a little path through the hedge in the back-yard. "It will take you right into Mr. Hardy's garden. If he's not busy, maybe he will show you what he grows."

Joey didn't care about the garden, but he was glad to go on the errand. He found the path through the hedge and pushed his way through to the other side. A big lawn lay in front of him. Nearby he saw a large green bush. It was shaped like a camel. Next to it was another bush that looked like a big green rooster. Scattered over the big lawn were all kinds of strange bushes.

Joey walked toward the green camel to look at it more closely.

Suddenly a deep voice called to him. "Watch where you're going, son!"

Joey stopped, startled. Then he saw a tall old man peering at him over the camel.

"You're stepping on my seedlings," the man said crossly.

Joey realized that the man was Mr. Hardy, and he was sorry that he hadn't been more careful.

Quickly Joey told Mr. Hardy
who he was and why he had come.

"Well, no harm done. You
stopped just in time," Mr.
Hardy said. "The hatchet is up
in the workshop. Come along."

On the way Mr. Hardy told

Joey about his bushes. "They
are called topiary bushes. I
clip and shape them as they
grow."

Mr. Hardy stopped in front of
a bush shaped like a round lady
and clipped her chin.

By the time Joey went home he and Mr. Hardy were good friends. Joey decided that growing things was interesting after all.

After lunch Joey worked in his own garden. He helped his grandmother cut tomato stakes.

"A new boy moved in across the street," Joey's grandmother told him. "He was going to help me, but he never showed up. You came to visit just in time."

The next morning Joey heard a strange noise way down the road. *Brup! Bzzz! Brrr!* It stopped. Then it started again. It sounded like an angry insect.

Joey went down the road under the big trees. At last he found

out what was making the noise.
A big truck stood in the road
ahead.

A strong steel arm rose above
the truck. Joey knew it was
called a cherry picker. He had
a toy at home just like it.

Joey saw a man at the top of the cherry picker. He was cutting off branches with a power saw high in the treetop. Three other men were working below.

Joey moved closer and closer to the truck. Finally he stood right under the man with the saw. Suddenly there was a loud noise overhead. *Crack!* Joey heard a shout and moved back just in time.

A big branch hit the ground where Joey had been standing.

"That was a close call!" one of the tree men exclaimed. He waved his hand at a sign with red flags. "Don't you see that danger sign? Go stand in back of it!"

Joey did what he was told right away.

Then Joey asked the tree man what he was doing.

"We're cutting down the tree. It has Dutch elm disease," the man told Joey. "See that yellow spot on the trunk? A tree expert puts it on to tell us that the tree is sick. When we see the mark we cut the tree down and burn it."

Joey saw the yellow spot and felt sad that the big tree was coming down.

Joey watched the man in the cherry picker. He cut off one branch after another. The three men below cut up the branches when they hit the ground. Next they heaped the wood in an empty lot. Then they set fire to the giant woodpile.

On the way home Joey noticed yellow spots on other tree trunks. Now he knew what they meant.

In front of his house Joey saw Mr. Hardy. He ran to tell him about the tree cutters.

Mr. Hardy nodded and frowned. "Dutch elm disease is caused by a fungus," he said. "The fungus is spread by the elm beetle when it flys from a sick tree to a healthy tree. If a tree gets sick, it must be cut down and burned."

The two of them were standing under the big elm tree in front of Joey's house as they talked.

"But this old elm is good and healthy!" Mr. Hardy exclaimed. "It's about the

biggest tree in town, and I spray
it along with my own."

Mr. Hardy pointed to the
next tree. "That tree is a maple.
It will stay healthy too. Maples
don't get Dutch elm disease,"
he explained.

The next morning the power saw sounded closer to Joey's house. Joey hurried up the road toward the noise. The tree cutters were just a block away. Big trees were cut down all along the road beyond the cherry picker. Joey saw bare white stumps where the big elms had stood. The tree men were starting to work on a new tree. Joey watched from behind the danger sign.

In a short time, a group of boys joined Joey. They were watching the tree cutters too.

After a while a boy with a striped shirt pushed another boy to one side. "Move over. You're in the way," he said.

"Cut it out, Billy," his friend answered, pushing him back.

Joey decided to stay away from Billy. He looked mean.

Soon a truck took a load of branches away.

"They're going to burn them! Cut and burn! Cut and burn!" Billy yelled. He seemed to like watching the trees come down.

Joey looked up to see what the power saw was doing in the tree. Suddenly he heard a hissing sound behind him and felt something cold on his arm. There was yellow paint all over him and on his shirt too.

Joey turned around and saw that Billy had a spray can in his hand. "Look what you've done!" he cried.

"It was an accident!" Billy exclaimed, laughing.

Joey was annoyed and decided to go home. On a fence near his house he saw the initials *W.G.* in big yellow letters. He wondered if Billy had sprayed them too.

When Joey got home, he told
his grandmother about Billy and
the spray can.

"He must be the new boy
across the street. His name is
Billy," she said. "Never mind.

Change your shirt and bring it to me."

Upstairs Joey heard noises down on the street. Out his window he saw Billy chasing someone with a can of spray paint.

The next morning a loud noise woke up Joey. *Brup! Bzzz! Brrr!* Joey looked out his window, but he couldn't believe what he saw. The cherry picker was under their giant elm tree. The men were getting ready to cut it down.

Joey dressed quickly and rushed outside. He waved to the tree men. "Wait! Don't cut that tree!" he shouted.

Joey ran toward the tree to talk to the men.

"That tree isn't sick," he cried.

The head tree man showed him a large yellow spot on the tree trunk. "It's marked for cutting," he said. "I'm sorry, son."

Joey knew that something was wrong. The yellow spot hadn't been on the elm tree yesterday, when he and Mr. Hardy had been talking about it.

Suddenly Joey saw the initials
W.G. sprayed in yellow on the
street. He pointed to them. "The
person who did that put the
spot on the elm tree," he told
the men.

The tree man rubbed his chin.
"Maybe so," he said.

Just then a clear voice called
from across the street. "William!
William Grant! I want this yellow paint off these steps before
your father sees it!"

As they watched Billy came around the corner and disappeared inside. Now they all knew who had painted the spot on the elm tree.

Joey showed the men that there was a yellow spot on the maple tree too. "Maples don't get Dutch elm disease," he said.

At that moment Mr. Hardy and Joey's grandmother appeared. The tree man told them about the near mistake.

Joey was glad that he had
acted quickly. The tree man was
pleased too.

"Thanks to this boy, you've
still got an elm tree," he said.
"He got to us just in time."